P9-BYZ-615

Property of
SELF School

A First-Start® Easy Reader

This easy reader contains only 41 different words, repeated often to help the young reader develop word recognition and interest in reading.

Basic word list for *Skating on Thin Ice*

all
always
and
any
at
best
but
cries
dizzy
fast
faster
Flo
getting
he
help
is
it
Joe
likes
look
now
out
Rosie
saves
she
skate
skates
slow
slower
smiles
sometimes
than
they
to
together
too
twirls
way
when
whirls
with

Skating on Thin Ice

Written by Louise Everett
Illustrated by Richard Max Kolding

Troll Associates

Library of Congress Cataloging in Publication Data

Everett, Louise.
Skating on thin ice.

Summary: In this easy-to-read story, Rosie the elephant and her friend Joe enjoy ice skating until Joe falls into the ice.
[1. Ice skating—Fiction. 2. Friendship—Fiction. 3. Elephants—Fiction] I. Kolding, Richard Max, ill. II. Title.
PZ7.E918Sk 1987 [E] 86-30857
ISBN 0-8167-0992-0 (lib. bdg.)
ISBN 0-8167-0993-9 (pbk.)

Copyright © by Troll Associates

All rights reserved. No portion of this book may be reproduced in any form, electronic or mechanical, including photocopying, recording, or information storage and retrieval systems, without prior written permission from the publisher.
Printed in the United States of America.

10 9 8 7

Rosie likes to skate.

She likes to skate fast.

She likes to skate slow.

She likes to skate any way at all.

Joe likes to skate, too.

He likes to skate fast.

He likes to skate slow.

He likes to skate any way at all.

Sometimes, Rosie skates
faster than Joe.

Sometimes, Joe skates
faster than Rosie.

Sometimes, Rosie skates
slower than Joe.

Sometimes, Joe skates slower than Rosie.

Rosie likes it best when
they skate together.

Flo likes to skate, too.

She likes to skate with Joe.

Flo smiles.

Joe smiles.

Flo whirls.

Joe twirls.

Joe whirls.

Joe twirls.

Joe is getting dizzy.

Look out, Joe!

DANGER

"Help," cries Joe.

“Help,” cries Flo.

Rosie saves Joe.

Now, Joe skates fast

and Joe skates slow . . .

but he always skates with Rosie.